D0601956

ELBERT'S BAD WORD

by Audrey Wood

illustrated by

Audrey and Don Wood

HARCOURT BRACE & COMPANY
San Diego   New York   London
Printed in Singapore

TO MARIA MODUGNO

Text copyright © 1988 by Audrey Wood
Illustrations copyright ©1988 by Audrey Wood and Don Wood

All rights reserved. No part of this publication may
be reproduced or transmitted in any form or by any means,
electronic or mechanical, including photocopy, recording, or
any information storage and retrieval system, without
permission in writing from the publisher.

Requests for permission to make copies
of any part of the work should be mailed to:
Permissions Department,
Harcourt Brace & Company,
6277 Sea Harbor Drive, Orlando, Florida 32887-6777.

Library of Congress Cataloging-in-Publication Data
Wood, Audrey.
Elbert's bad word.
Summary:
After shocking the elegant garden party by using a bad word,
Elbert learns some acceptable substitutes from a helpful wizard.
[1. Swearing—Fiction.   2. Magicians—Fiction.]
I. Title.   II. Series.
PZ7.W846E1   1988   (E)   86-7557
ISBN 0-15-225320-3
ISBN 0-15-201367-9 pb
G I K M O P N L J H

Printed in Singapore

The illustrations in this book were first drawn in pencil by Audrey Wood
and then rendered in color by Don Wood in watercolor, gouache, and
colored pencils on coquille board.
The text type was set in Bernhard Modern by Thompson Type, San Diego, California.
Printed and bound by Tien Wah Press, Singapore
Production supervision by Warren Wallerstein and Rebecca Miller
Designed by Nancy J. Ponichtera

One afternoon at an elegant garden party,

young Elbert heard a word he had never heard before.

The word floated by like a small storm cloud.
It was ugly and covered with dark, bristly hairs. With
a swift flick of his wrist, Elbert snatched the word from
the air and stuffed it into his back pocket.

Forgetting about it, the boy went on his way. But the word waited patiently. When Aunt Isabella sang opera in soprano,

the word made itself small and flew into Elbert's mouth
like a little gnat.

That's when the trouble began. Chives the Butler tried to balance too many trays of deviled eggs.

He dropped them all onto Madame Friatta's gown.

Madame Friatta spilled her spritzer on Sir Hilary's bald head.

Sir Hilary threw his croquet mallet up into the air.

Then, with a terrible thud, the mallet landed on Elbert's great toe. Elbert opened his mouth to scream, but the bad word sprang out, bigger and uglier than before.

Everyone at the party was shocked. They couldn't believe their ears.

"Come with me, young man!" Elbert's mother said with a frown. The word made itself small again, about the size of a rat, and followed in the boy's shadow.

In the lavatory Elbert's mother handed him a bar of soap.

"We do not say bad words," she said. "Clean it out of your mouth, and never use it again!" While Elbert scrubbed his tongue, the bad word sat on his shoulder, snickering wickedly.

Elbert knew something had to be done.

He ran down a cobbled path, past the reflecting pool,
beyond the gazebo, and knocked at the gardener's cottage.
The gardener, who was also a practicing wizard, opened
the door with a smile.

"Come in," he said, "and bring that thing with you."

The wizard gardener knew right away that Elbert had
caught a bad word and needed a cure. Opening his desk, he
pulled out a drawer filled with words that crackled and sparkled.
"Sometimes we need strong words," he said, "to say how we
feel. Use these, and perhaps you won't get into trouble."

Taking the sparkling words from the drawer, the wizard gardener tossed them in a bowl with flour and honey. He added some raisins, milk, and eggs, mixed them all together, then baked a little cake.

The cake was delicious, so Elbert ate every last crumb. And as he did, the ugly word shriveled to the size of a flea and hopped onto his necktie.

Everyone was enjoying Cousin Rudolph's oboe solo in
D minor when Elbert returned to the party.

But soon the trouble began anew.

Chives the butler tripped on Madame Friatta's feathered boa.

Madame Friatta dropped her chocolate mousse on
Sir Hilary's bald head.

Sir Hilary threw his croquet mallet up into the air.

Then, with a terrible thud, the mallet landed on
Elbert's great toe.

The music stopped.

Everyone stared at the boy.

Elbert's face grew red with anger.

"MY STARS! THUNDER AND LIGHTNING!
RATS AND BLUE BLAZES! SUFFERING CATS!
BLISTERING HOP TOADS! ZOUNDS AND
GADZOOKS!" he shouted.

Everyone breathed a sigh of relief and gave Elbert
three rousing cheers . . .

. . . but no one was more pleased than Elbert. As the music
began again, he saw something that looked like a little spider
scurry down a dark hole, and disappear.

3 1221 07880 2621